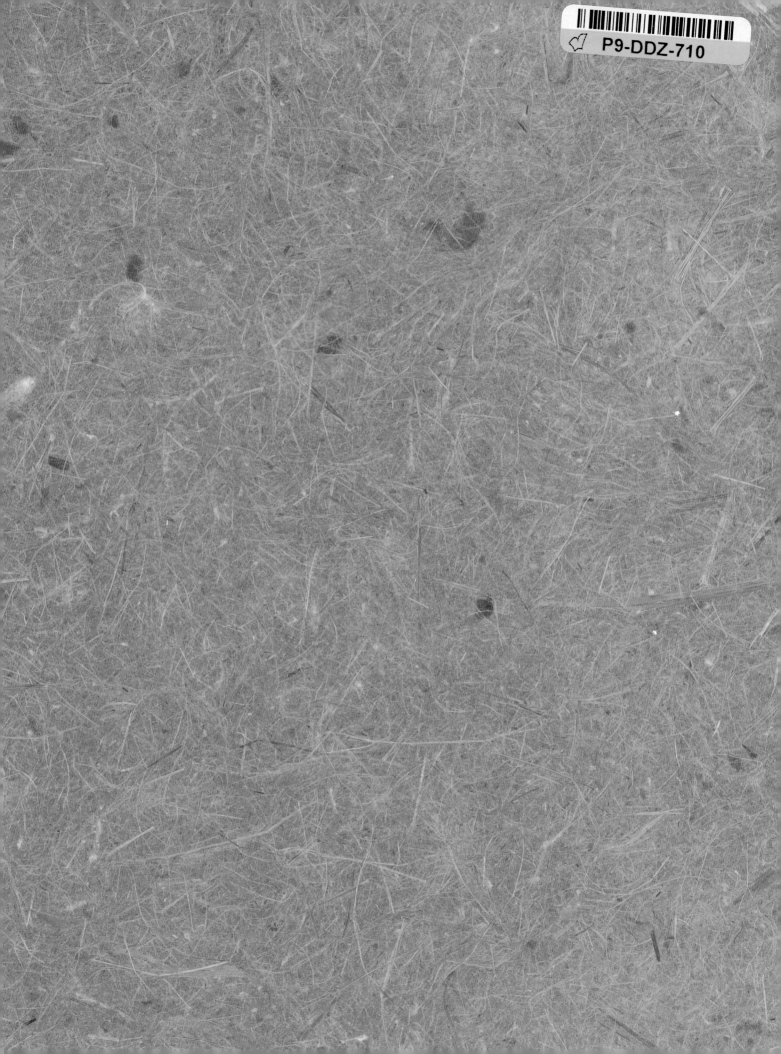

P9-DDZ-710

Moontellers

MYTHS OF THE MOON FROM AROUND THE WORLD

by
LYNN MORONEY

illustrated by
GREG SHED

Northland Publishing

To Michael Thomas Finn Moroney, himself.

I want to thank and acknowledge my editor, Erin Murphy,
whose patience and vision brought this book to completion.
—L. M.

To Lila and Jim, my parents, for all of their support over the years.
—G. S.

The illustrations in this book were done in oils and colored pencils on canvas

The display type was set in Ovidius

The text type was set in Bembo

Composed by Northland Publishing, Flagstaff, Arizona

Printed and bound by South Sea International Press, Ltd., in Hong Kong

Production supervision by Lisa Brownfield

Art direction and cover design by Trina Stahl

Interior design by Rudy J. Ramos

Editing by Erin Murphy

FIRST EDITION

ISBN 0-87358-601-8

Library of Congress Catalog Card Number 95-2418

Cataloging-in-Publication Data

Moroney, Lynn.

Moontellers : myths of the moon from around the world / Lynn Moroney ;
illustrated by Greg Shed. — 1st ed.

p. cm.

Includes bibliographical references.

ISBN 0-87358-601-8 : $14.95

1. Moon—Folklore. 2. Moon—Mythology. [1. Moon—Folklore.] I. Shed, Greg, ill. II. Title.

GR625.M67 1995

398.26—dc20   95-2418

[E]

507/10M/5-95

Moontellers

Are all the people

Who tell us about the moon.

They enchant us with folklore and facts,

And on wonder–full–moon nights, they tell

Us wonderful moon stories.

How grand, the world has

Moontellers.

Moon Man

EUAHLAYI, AUSTRALIA

LONG AGO IN THE Dreamtime, Baloo the Moon decided to visit earth. He soon came upon two maidens standing by a river, and they invited him to ride in their canoe. When he stepped into the little boat, it rocked and tipped, and then *splash!* Baloo fell into the dark water. The girls laughed.

This embarrassed Baloo. He fled home, and for a few days he stayed hidden from sight. Slowly he grew round and bright and full of courage, and he returned to earth. But when he remembered the girls and how they laughed, he began to shrink away. Every month Baloo grows round and proud and bright, and every month he remembers his fall and shrinks away.

———

THE EUAHLAYI (YOU-AH-LAY-EE) IS one of the many tribes of Aborigines, the first people of Australia. Each Aboriginal tribe has its own traditions, customs, and stories, but all tribes have at least one thing in common. They all tell about the Dreamtime, a time when human-like creatures walked about Australia, learning how to get along with one another. In time, the people of the Dreamtime turned into the special landmarks of Australia.

Today, Aboriginal elders guide young people on "walkabouts" so they may learn the stories and rituals of their tribes. In this way, the elders pass on the mystery and wisdom of the Dreamtime.

Ask the sandpainters in Australia,
What do you see in the moon?
They'll tell you they see a man in the moon.
The sandpainters tell of Baloo.

Rabbit and Frog

CHINA

ONE NIGHT LADY HENG-O found a small vial containing the Water of Life. She was seized with a great thirst and immediately drank the magic liquid. With the first sip, she began to whirl and spin about, and then went flying up into the starry heavens, holding the vial in her hand. When Lady Heng-O reached the moon, the water spilled and turned into a white jade rabbit, and the noble lady turned into a lowly frog.

Now when you look at the full moon, you can see Lady Frog sitting at the feet of Moon Rabbit, waiting as he mixes and crushes moon herbs with his mortar and pestle. He is trying to make a magic potion that will return them to earth, but he has not yet succeeded.

IN CHINA'S ANCIENT TIMES, the moon was called the Pearl of Heaven. Chinese astronomers were held in high esteem, and they often advised the emperors in times of trouble. The star maps and records made by those scholars have contributed greatly to our knowledge of the universe.

Each autumn the Chinese people celebrate the harvest with a Moon Festival. Beautiful paper lanterns give a magical glow to the festivities. The people eat rice cakes, round and white like the moon; exchange gifts; and tell the story of the Moon Rabbit and Lady Frog.

Ask the dragon dancers in China,
What do you see in the moon?
They'll tell you they see a rabbit and a frog.
The dragon dancers tell of Heng-O.

Weaver and Cat

IROQUOIS, NORTH AMERICA

ONCE AN OLD WOMAN went to live on the moon. There, with her pet wildcat looking on, she began to weave a headband. As the weaving grew longer, the moon grew larger. Soon the weaving was finished and the moon was full.

But when the old woman looked away to stir some corn in a pot, that little cat pounced! He pawed and clawed, and as he slowly unraveled the weaving, the moon disappeared. The old weaver and the old moon had to begin anew, as they do every month even to this time.

IN TRADITIONAL IROQUOIS SOCIETY, each clan was headed by a woman and was housed under the roof of one giant "longhouse," often bigger than a football field. The clan mothers appointed, advised, and dismissed chiefs; controlled possessions; and supervised the raising of the children and the planting and harvesting. They were likened to the "Three Sisters" (corn, beans, and squash), because their wisdom and strength nourished and sustained the Iroquois people.

Clans formed the building blocks of the Mohawk, Oneida, Onondaga, Cayuga, and Seneca nations. The nations in turn formed the remarkable Confederacy of the Iroquois, a group that joined to maintain the Great Peace. Years later, this confederacy was used as a model to form another nation, the United States of America.

Ask the Clan Mothers of the Iroquois,
What do you see in the moon?
They'll tell you they see a woman and cat.
The Clan Mothers tell of a weaver.

Moon Woman

POLYNESIA

ONE NIGHT, WHILE ON her way to gather water, Hina stopped to watch a full moon rise from the sea. The bright moon formed a night rainbow that stretched to the top of the starry sky. Hina had long wished to live in the heavens, so she stepped onto the rainbow and walked all the way to the moon.

She lives there now. All night she beats and pounds tree bark on her tapa board, making the cloth that she uses to form the clouds that cover the earth.

THE ISLANDS OF POLYNESIA lie within the great triangle formed in the Pacific Ocean by New Zealand, Hawaii, and Easter Island. Polynesian navigators invented a way of using the positions of the rising and setting stars to know their locations as they sailed for days at a time in the long stretches between islands. When they traveled, they took their ancient tales with them in the form of long poems and songs they had memorized.

Though she has many names (Hina, Ina, Sina, Rona), and though there are many versions of how and why she went to the moon, all Polynesians tell stories of the woman in the moon.

Ask the night singers in the South Seas,
What do you see in the moon?
They'll tell you they see Hina, Maker of Clouds.
The night singers tell of their moon mother.

Rabbit

AZTECS, MEXICO

IN THE TIME WHEN the world was dark, the ancient gods asked, "Who will jump into our fire and become our sun, so we may have light?" Only one god had the courage to jump into the roaring fire. He cast himself into the flames, and at once he flew into the sky and became the sun.

Another god, jealous of the praise given to the sun, threw himself into the fire; he also shot into the sky, becoming a second sun. There was now too much light. This angered the gods, and one of them threw a rabbit at the second sun's face, dimming his light and turning him into the moon. You can still see the imprint of the rabbit on his face today.

THE SUN AND MOON play an important part in the history and art of Mexico. In ancient times, builders erected pyramids to the sun and moon. These pyramids were still standing when the Aztecs established the most powerful empire ever known in Mexico. Advanced in the study of astronomy and math, the Aztecs assembled architects, political leaders, physicians, artists, and craftspeople to construct a great city in the Valley of Mexico.

Mexico is now a democracy, but the descendents of the Aztecs continue to create works of art, crafts, and literature that reflect one of the richest heritages in Mexico.

Ask the maskmakers in Mexico,
What do you see in the moon?
They'll tell you they see the rabbit tossed there.
The maskmakers tell of a Moon Rabbit.

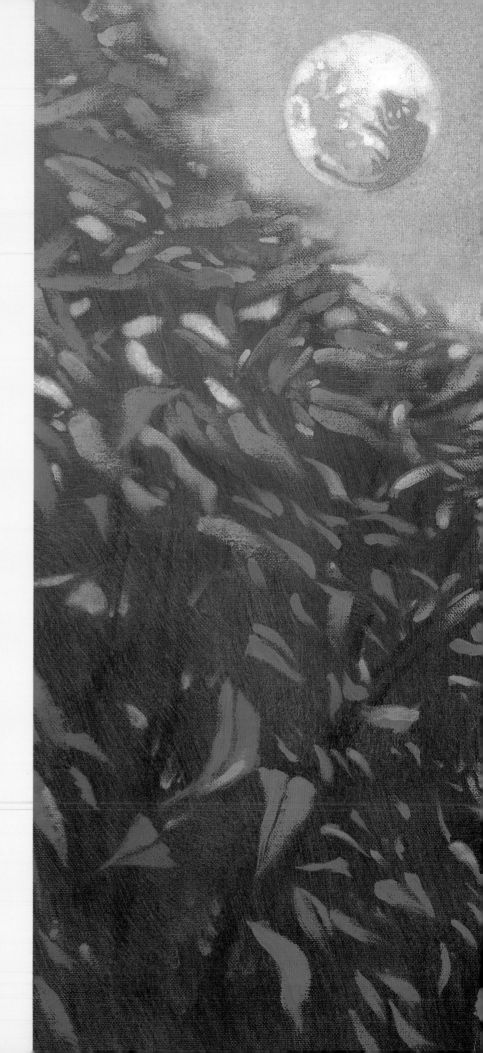

Four-Eyed Jaguar

YURACARE, BOLIVIA

LONG AGO, THE GREAT hunter Tiri shot an arrow at a small animal called a paca. The paca cried, "Why do you hunt the small creatures? We have never harmed you. You should hunt the four-eyed jaguar, for he is cruel to all the people and animals."

Tiri began to hunt for the evil jaguar, who could see everything with his two pairs of eyes and always knew when Tiri was near. At last Tiri came upon him hiding in the top of a tree. The jaguar could not escape. He cried out, "Animals, save me! Trees, save me! Stars, save me!" Just then he saw the moon. "Moon, save me!" he cried, hurling himself up to live forever on the moon.

ON THE EASTERN SLOPES of the Andes Mountains in Bolivia, South America, live the Yuracare (yur-ah-CAH-ray) people. Long ago, Yuracare adults fished, cultivated small crops, wove cloth, made pottery, and slept in hammocks while children played games and made string figures. As with many cultures, the Yuracare passed on their history and traditions by telling stories.

The ways of the rain forest peoples are rapidly changing, for each day hundreds of trees disappear from their forest home. The trees of the great rain forests place oxygen into the air we breathe. Many people ask, "What will happen to the world when the rain forests have been cut away?"

Ask the forest people in Bolivia,
What do you see in the moon?
They'll tell you they see the four-eyed jaguar.
The forest people tell of a jaguar.

Bare-Legged Boy

LOUCHEUX, CANADA

LONG AGO, A CLEVER boy was always using magic to get what he wanted. The elders warned him that he was too young to know the power of his magic, but the boy paid no attention.

The boy began to watch how the moon could change shape and move through the sky. He admired the powers of the moon, and one night he wished himself there. As the elders had told him, his magic was too strong, and he shot up and out through the smoke hole of his house, tearing his pant leg along the way.

Now, when the moon rises into the sky full and round as a drum, the boy stands there with a bare leg for all to see.

———

THE LOUCHEUX (LOO-shoo) LIVE in the Canadian subarctic region, which stretches across the Northwest Territories and the Yukon Territory into Alaska. Here the summers are as warm as 90 degrees Fahrenheit and the winters reach 50 degrees below zero.

In the ancient time of the moon boy, the Loucheux survived the cold winter by wearing warm clothing made of caribou skins, and insulating their round shelters with packed snow. They hunted for moose, mountain sheep, and caribou in sleds or snowshoes. Today their daily lives are made easier by modern inventions like snowmobiles and electric heat, but many of the traditional ways live on, along with the magical stories of long ago.

Ask the hunters in the far, far north,
What do you see in the moon?
They'll tell you they see a bare-legged boy.
The hunters tell of a moon boy.

Boy and Girl with a Pail

SCANDINAVIA

HJUKI (EE-YUH-KEE) AND HIS sister, Bil (BEEL), were forced to work day and night gathering water from a magic well. One night Moon saw the children, and, filled with pity, he took them to live in his house.

The children are happy living on the moon, for now they gather water but once a month. When the moon is full, they are seen with a bucket and pole. Over a few nights, Hjuki falls out of sight. Later on, Bil disappears. The moon is soon dark and empty. In a few days, the moon begins to fill, and the children may be seen once more, first Hjuki, then Bil.

———

THE VIKINGS WERE ADVENTURERS known for their bravery at sea. They sailed the Atlantic Ocean and found a "new land," but they did not stay, and it would be many years before Europeans would again visit North America.

Scandinavia has given the world great poets and storytellers, such as Snorri Sturluson, who recorded the old tales like the one above, and Hans Christian Andersen, who wrote stories familiar to us all.

You may have heard a different version of Hjuki and Bil's story: "Jack and Jill went up the hill to fetch a pail of water . . ."

Ask the Vikings in Scandinavia,

What do you see in the moon?

They'll tell you they see a boy and girl with a pail.

The Vikings tell of Hjuki and Bil.

Handprints

INDIA

ASTANGI MATA WAS THE mother of all that lived and grew on the earth, but the sky was empty. She loved her children, the twins Chanda and Suraj, and decided to give them everlasting life as rulers of the heavens.

Astangi Mata told Suraj, "You shall be the Raja of the Sky—ever-hot, nurturer of growing things," and Suraj twirled up into the sky. Then she turned to Chanda, saying, "You shall be the moon—cool, ever-changing, new, and beautiful," and Chanda started her journey skyward. Too late, Astangi Mata reached out to embrace her daughter one last time, and she could but caress Chanda's cheek. The beautiful Moon bears her mother's handprints even to this time.

THE PEOPLES OF INDIA pay close attention to the moon, for it is the moon calendar that determines the dates of their many festivals and celebrations. Most celebrations are religious occasions, but some street parades, led by musicians, celebrate family events such as weddings and funerals. India is a land of festivals.

India gave the world one of the greatest men of this century, Mohadas Gandhi. He worked so that today's Indians, so long ruled by others, can now rule themselves.

Ask the musicians in India,
What do you see in the moon?
They'll tell you they see a mother's handprints.
The musicians tell of Astangi Mata.

Brush Burner

COWBOYS, UNITED STATES

ONE MORNING WHEN THE moon was just setting over the prairie, Cooky said, "Looky there! Someone's burnin' brush on the moon!" Two of the cowboys began to argue about whether it was a man or a woman doing the burning. Soon they were shouting back and forth, and the herd began to moo and mill around.

At last the trail boss cried, "Y'all hush! You'll cause a stampede, and this herd'll run from here to that moon you're arguin' about." That ended the discussion right then and there, but for the rest of the drive, those cowboys never did agree about who was burning brush on the moon.

THE AMERICAN COWBOY GREW to fame during the time of the great cattle drives in the latter part of the 1800s, when thousands of cattle were rounded up, branded, and moved from Texas to the railroads of Kansas. Cowboys took turns watching the herd at night, knowing when to relieve each other by using the Big Dipper as a clock.

Cowboys entertained one another with stories and songs. Storytelling remains a part of cowboy life, and now cowboy poets sing and tell story-poems that entertain us all.

Ask the cowboys out in the West,
What do you see in the moon?
They'll tell you they see someone
*   burning brush.*
The cowboys tell of a brush burner.

Drummer

GOURO, CÔTE D'IVOIRE

YOUNG AND OLD GATHERED in the center of the compound. They visited and danced and sang the clapping songs. The full moon was rising and it was getting late as the people grew quiet. An elder spoke: "In the moon sits the drummer. He plays his drum, his talking drum. He plays for our ancestors. When our people die, they go to the sky and live on the moon. While you sleep, dreaming one dream, another dream, and then one more, your ancestors listen to the drum and watch over you to keep you safe. All is well now. Go to sleep."

DURING THE DAY IN Africa's République de Côte d'Ivoire (Republic of the Ivory Coast), the Gouro (goo-ROE) people farm the flat land, hunt in the forests, and cook meals in the mud houses of their family compounds. At night, they gather in the center of the compounds to share the day's events and to hear stories, often told by dancing and using hand motions along with the sounds of "talking drums."

These drums don't just keep a beat. They form sounds like actual words. Drummers must study long to learn the language of the drum—only then are they able to sound out words and sentences to carry on the stories of their people.

Ask the old ones in Africa,

What do you see in the moon?

They'll tell you they see a drummer man.

The old ones tell of the drummer.

Moon Seas

ASTRONOMERS, WORLDWIDE

BILLIONS OF YEARS AGO, gigantic space objects called meteors slammed into the moon. They punched deep holes and sent matter sloshing up the sides of the holes to form rings of high mountains. These "moonpocks" are called impact craters.

When the largest meteors (some as large as a mountain!) struck the young hot moon, they cracked its surface. Moon lava flowed up and out of the cracks and spread across large areas of the moon's surface. In time the lava cooled and turned dark. It was in this way that the dark patches called "seas" were formed on the moon.

WHEN THE ASTRONAUTS WALKED on the Sea of Tranquillity in 1969, they saw craters no larger than a teacup. These impact craters were formed many millions of years after the seas by pebble-size meteors, such as those we see streaking through our night sky.

Astronomy is sometimes called the "mother of science" because from the earliest of times, people have studied and recorded the comings and goings of heavenly bodies.

The story of the moon is not yet finished. When astronomers and other scientists learn something new about the moon, they are quick to tell all the world.

Ask astronomers anywhere in the world,
What do you see in the moon?
They'll tell you they see mountains and seas.
The astronomers tell of moon craters.

Ask yourself some full moon night,
What do you see in the moon?
Tell what you see to your family and friends,
And you'll be a Moonteller, too.

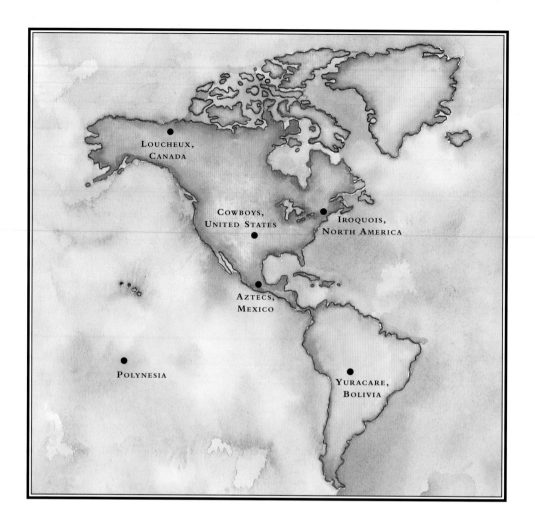

A Note from the Author

BECAUSE OF THE MOTION and position of the moon relative to earth, some moon pictures are seen when the moon is rising, while others are best seen when the moon is overhead or setting. Hence, when one picture is "just right," another might look upside-down. Not to be outdone by the moon, the illustrator has used some tricks of his own and drawn the moon so that you can best see the pictures, no matter their time and place.

In the ancient times, people thought the moon was magic. Today, superstitions about the moon—indeed, the universe—have been replaced with something even more wonderful: mystery. The mysteries of the universe prompt the work of storytellers and scientists, and it is they who invite us to celebrate the world, learn how it works, and discover how humankind can live in peace and share in its many gifts. May this book invite you to enter into a few of the mysteries of the universe, so that you may discover the even greater mysteries that are a part of you.

Here is a map to guide you in further exploration of the cultures in this book, and a list of sources to light the way.

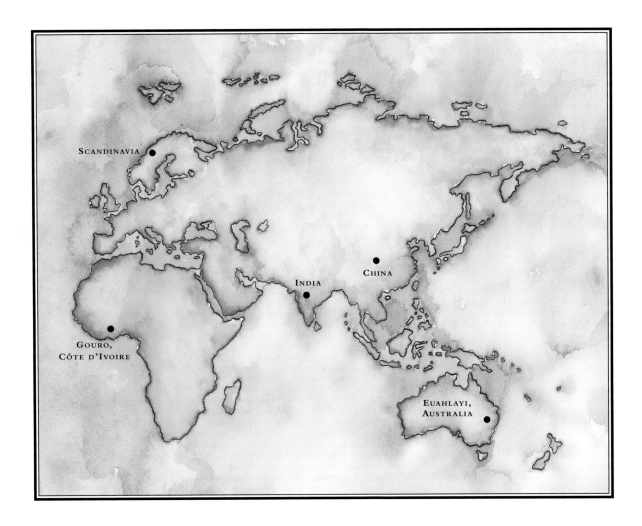

Story Sources and Further Reading

Euahlayi, Australia—K. Langloh Parker. *Australian Legendary Tales* (Sydney: Angus and Robertson, 1953).

China—Donald MacKenzie, *China and Japan* (London: Studio Editions Ltd., 1986).

Iroquois, North America—E. A. Smith, *Myths of the Iroquois* (1883; reprint, Oswheken, Ontario: Iroqrafts Ltd., 1989).

Polynesia—Johannes C. Anderson, *Myths and Legends of the Polynesians* (Rutland: Charles E. Tuttle Company, 1969).

Aztecs, Mexico—Irene Nicholson, *Mexican and Central American Mythology* (London: Hamlyn, 1967); Bradley Smith, *Mexico: A History in Art* (New York: Doubleday and Company, 1968); and Charles R. Wicke, "The Mezoamerican Rabbit in the the Moon: An Influence from Han China?" in *Archeaoastronomy* 7 (1984).

Yuracare, Bolivia—Alfred Metraux, "Tribes of the eastern slopes of the Bolivian Andes," in *Handbook of South American Indians* 3, ed. Julian H. Steward (Washington, D.C.: U.S. Government Printing Office, 1948).

Loucheux, Canada—C. M. Barbeau, ed., "Loucheux Myths," in *Journal of American Folklore* 28 (1916); and Carl Waldman, *Encyclopedia of Native American Tribes* (New York: Facts on File, 1988).

Scandinavia—Snorri Sturlson, *The Prose Edda*, trans. Jean I. Young (Berkeley: University of California Press, 1964).

India—Verrier Elwin, *Myths of Middle India* (Oxford: Oxford University Press, 1991); and Catherine A. Galbraith and Rama Mehta, *India, Now and Through Time* (New York: Houghton-Mifflin, 1980).

Cowboys, United States—Frank J. Dobie, *A Vaquero of the Brush Country* (1929; reprint, Dallas: Southwest Press, 1971).

Guoro, Côte d'Ivoire—Many Africans have told me of the drummer in the moon. My informant for this version was Paule-Laurence Fezan, a Gouroan student at Oklahoma City University. She learned of the drummer from her grandmother, who lives in Côte d'Ivoire. Thank you, Lulu!

Astronomers, Worldwide—Michael Zeilik, *Astronomy: The Evolving Universe,* 5th ed. (New York: John Wiley & Sons, 1988).

Check your library for other books that have moon stories you might enjoy, including *The Moon Is a Crystal Ball: Unfamiliar Legends of the Stars,* by Natalia Belting (Indianapolis: The Bobbs-Merrill Company, Inc., 1952); *Thirteen Moons on Turtle's Back,* by Joseph Bruchac (New York: Philomel, 1992); *Moon Lore,* by Timothy Harley (Rutland, Vermont: Charles E. Tuttle Co., 1970); *The Man in the Moon,* by Alta Jablow and Carl Withers (New York: Holt, Rinehart, & Winston, 1969); and *The Moon and You,* by E. C. Krupp (New York: Macmillan, 1993).

About the Author and Illustrator

David Fitzgerald

LYNN MORONEY fell in love with the sky as a child on the Oklahoma prairie—the heavens are as important to prairie dwellers as the sea, mountains, or forests are to people living elsewhere. In her five years with the Kirkpatrick Planetarium in Oklahoma City, Lynn began gathering legends about the sun, moon, stars, and sky, and she is now a professional storyteller and writer specializing in sky lore. She has previously had three books published—*Baby Rattlesnake* and *Elinda Who Danced in the Sky* (Children's Book Press), and *The Boy Who Loved Bears* (Children's Press)—and has produced three audio cassettes of sky stories. Lynn calls herself "a true Okie"—a citizen of the Chickasaw Nation who has lived most her life in the state of Oklahoma.

Jim Shed

GREG SHED grew up in California, where instead of surfing like all of his friends, he taught himself to paint. He worked for many years as a commercial artist, with such clients as Disney and Pepsi-Cola, before becoming a children's book illustrator. *Moontellers,* published in the year of Greg's twentieth anniversary as an artist, is the third book he has illustrated. His first, *Casey Over There* (Harcourt Brace), was included in the prestigious New York Society of Illustrators' 1994 show. Greg lives in his native San Diego with his wife, Sharon, who assists with his exhaustive research—even making occasional costumes for his models—and who has herself modeled for two of his books.